Not Too Small After All

Not Too Small

After All

by ELEANOR CLYMER

Pictures by TOM O'SULLIVAN

FRANKLIN WATTS, Inc.
699 Madison Ave.   New York 21

To Bobby

Not Too Small After All

It was Saturday morning, a fine day in spring. Joey
was sitting on the front porch of his new house hugging
a basketball and feeling very happy.

He was happy for a number of reasons. First of all,

1

here he was, living right next door to his cousin Jim. Joey wanted to be just like Jim. When Joey had lived in the city he could see Jim only once in a long while. But now he could see him every day.

Jim was big and strong and had tough muscles. He could do everything. He could play basketball and baseball and he could ride a bike and swim and—well, everything. So, living right next door to him, Joey figured he could learn to do those things too. Jim was eleven and a half, three and a half years older than Joey. But Joey didn't mind that. He and Jim were good friends and Jim would surely help him.

And there was another reason why Joey was happy. When he and his mother and father were packing up to move, they had found a lot of interesting things in a basement storeroom of their apartment house. There were a fishing rod and a baseball glove and this basketball and some other things packed away in a crate.

"Where did all those things come from, Pop?" Joey had asked his father.

"Oh, I used them when I was younger," said his father. "But I haven't had time lately. And there's no room for them in the apartment, so your mother had me put them down here."

"May I use them when we get to our new house?" Joey asked.

"Of course," said his father. "As soon as you get big enough. You're too small now for that stuff."

4

"Oh, I'll soon be big enough," said Joey, and he helped his father carry out the crate just to show he was big enough to be of some use right away.

There had been several busy days while they were getting settled. Joey and his father helped Mother put things in place in their new house, and then Joey had to get registered in the new school. But on Saturday he had some free time at last. After breakfast he went up to the

5

attic where the crate was kept now. He took out the basket-ball and carried it downstairs.

"Where are you going with that basketball?" his mother asked.

"Out to play with Jim," said Joey.

"You're too small to handle that ball," said his mother.

"Pop said I could," said Joey.

"Well, all right," said his mother. "If Jim will take care of you."

Joey didn't quite like to be told that Jim had to *take care* of him, but he didn't let it bother him long. He sat on the porch and waited for Jim to appear. Pretty soon he came out.

"Hi, Jim," said Joey, jumping off the porch and climbing through the hedge into Jim's yard.

"Hi, Joey," said Jim.

"What are you going to do?" Joey asked.

"Some of the boys are coming over," said Jim.

"May I play with you?" Joey asked. "I have this basket-ball."

"Well, I don't know," said Jim, doubtfully. "I'll see what the fellows say."

Pretty soon there was a sound of feet on the sidewalk, and along came four boys.

"This is my cousin Joey," said Jim. "Joey, this is Chuck. This is Bill, this is Johnny, this is Hank."

"Hi, Joey," said the boys.

"He wants to play with us," said Jim.

The four boys looked doubtfully down at Joey.

"He's pretty small," said Chuck.

Joey looked up at the boys. He didn't feel small. To himself he felt just right. "We could play with my basketball," he said.

"Well, all right," said Bill, "let's play kickball."

Just then a small brown dog came running along the pavement. It stopped at Jim's gate and barked.

"Hey, Chuck," said Jim, "Trixie followed you again."

Chuck went to the gate and let the dog in.

"You're a bad girl," he said. "I told you to stay home."

The dog wagged her tail.

"She won't stay home because my kid sister teases her," he explained. "She wants to come with me all the time."

Trixie ran around sniffing at all the boys and wagging her tail. She trotted up to Joey and gave him a good sniffing as if she wanted to get acquainted. Joey patted her smooth brown head and she stuck out her pink tongue and licked him.

"Go sit down, Trixie," Chuck told her.

Trixie sat down obediently right in the middle of the

9

yard. Chuck took her by the collar and led her off to one
side.

"Stay there!" he ordered.

Bill marked out the field for kickball and Jim was
pitcher. Chuck was up first. Jim rolled the ball to him.
Chuck gave it a mighty kick. It soared over Jim's head

into the outfield. Joey ran with his arms outstretched to catch it. The ball bounced against his chest and knocked him flat. Before Joey could get to his feet the ball rolled to the edge of the yard. Trixie jumped up and ran after it, barking excitedly. Chuck ran around the bases and made a home run.

11

"What happened, Joey?" Jim asked. "Why didn't you catch it?"

"I guess he's too small," said Bill.

"Well, we'll give him another chance," said Jim. "Okay, Joey, you can be up now."

Joey took his place at home plate. Jim rolled the ball. Joey gave it a kick—the hardest he could manage—but before he got halfway to first base Jim had caught the ball.

"You're out!" Jim called, while Trixie jumped up and down and barked loudly.

"Gosh, we'll never get anywhere this way," said Chuck. "Trixie barks and Joey can't play."

"He's just too small," said Johnny.

"No, I'm not," said Joey.

"Yes, you are," said Jim. "You go over there and watch."

Joey walked over to the hedge and sat down. The boys went on playing.

Suddenly a cold little nose poked itself into his ear. It was Trixie. She wagged her tail.

12

She seemed to be saying, "Maybe you'll pay some attention to me."

Joey put his arm around her and patted her warm silky coat. Then he jumped up.

"Come on," he said to Trixie. "We'll go and play in my yard."

He took her by the collar and led her through the hedge. He got a rubber ball and threw it for her to catch. She dashed after it and caught it and ran back to Joey, wagging her tail. Joey threw it again and again. Trixie barked happily.

13

At last she wouldn't run any more. She stood and looked up at Joey with her tongue hanging out.

"I guess you want a drink," said Joey.

He brought a dish of water and put it on the ground. Trixie lapped it up thirstily, making a lot of noise about it.

Then Joey brought some crackers and she sat up on her hind legs and begged for them.

14

When the boys in Jim's yard had to go home for lunch,
Joey was sorry. He hadn't played much ball, but he'd had
fun with Trixie. He was sorry to see her go.

"So long, Joey. Thanks for taking care of Trixie," said
Chuck.

Jim came over into Joey's yard and they practiced
throwing and catching the basketball for a while.

"When you get bigger, you'll be pretty good at this," said Jim.

Joey thought he wasn't bad at it right now, but he didn't say anything. He decided he'd just keep on trying till the boys saw that he could play as well as anyone.

The next Saturday morning Joey was out early sitting on the porch. Pretty soon Jim came out. This time he was carrying a fishing pole and a can of bait.

"Hi, Jim," said Joey.

"Hi, Joey," said Jim.

"Where you going?" Joey asked.

"Fishing with the fellows."

"Can I come?"

"Oh, no, Joey, you're too small," said Jim.

"Oh, please," said Joey. "I'm not too small."

"But you haven't any fishing tackle."

"Yes, I have," said Joey. "You wait." He ran up to the attic, opened the crate and got out the rod and reel. He carried them downstairs.

"Where are you going?" his mother asked.

"Fishing with the fellows," said Joey.

"Oh, no," said his mother. "You're too small to go fishing. Anyway, that's your father's rod."

"He said I could use it when I got big enough, and I am," said Joey. "Jim is going."

"Well, all right," said his mother doubtfully. "If Jim will help you."

Joey hurried out before his mother had a chance to change her mind. He ran over to Jim's yard.

17

"Here I am," he said.

Jim didn't look very pleased. "I didn't say you could come, did I?" he asked.

"You said I had no fishing tackle," said Joey. "But I have."

Jim looked at the rod.

"It's a good one," he admitted. "Is it yours?"

"It's my father's," said Joey. "But I can use it if you show me how."

"Now, look, Joey—" Jim began.

But just then there was a sound of feet on the pavement, and the loud happy barking of a little dog. Chuck, Bill, and Johnny came down the street. Trixie ran ahead of them.

She jumped up at Joey and tried to kiss him. She was glad to see him. But the boys were not.

"Is he going?" they asked Jim.

"He wants to," said Jim. "Should we let him?"

"No, he's too small," said Bill.

"Oh, *please*," Joey begged.

18

"But what do you know about fishing?" Johnny asked.

"Well, I could learn," said Joey.

They all looked at Jim. After all, Joey was Jim's cousin.

"Oh, well, all right," said Jim. "Let's give him a chance."

"All right, but he better keep quiet. He might scare the fish."

They walked to the creek. The water tumbled downhill over mossy rocks. Trees and bushes shaded it on both sides. In one place there was a quiet pool with a grassy

bank sloping down to it. Here the boys spread out their tackle. Jim showed Joey how to put a worm on his hook. Then they started fishing.

Joey stood at the edge of the stream, dangling his hook in the water. For a long time he stood there waiting for the fish to bite, but the fish were busy somewhere else. Trixie ran up and down the bank sniffing, and then lay down to take a nap in the sun. Joey was beginning to get sleepy too, when suddenly something gave a strong pull on his line. It nearly jerked the rod out of his hands.

"Hey! Help!" Joey shouted. "I caught a fish!"

Trixie jumped up and began to bark.

Joey tried to pull his hook out of the water, but the fish swam away, unwinding the line.

"Reel it in! Reel it in!" Jim shouted.

Joey tried to turn the little handle of the reel, but the fish was too strong for him. It leaped and jerked, broke the line, and was gone. Trixie jumped in front of Joey and tripped him, and down he went into the water, letting go of the rod.

"Help! It's floating away!" he shouted.

Jim jumped in and rescued the rod, and Trixie, greatly excited, jumped in after him. The water wasn't deep, and they soon climbed out, but they were good and wet. Trixie ran around shaking herself and spraying all the boys with water.

"Stop that, Trixie!" said Chuck. "Go home now!"

But Trixie just grinned at him and wagged her tail.

"Why don't you tie her up at home?" Johnny asked.

"Oh, my kid sister would pester her," said Chuck. "Come on, let's get some fish."

But the water was all muddy where Joey and Trixie had fallen in.

"We'll have to go upstream," said Jim. "Listen, Joey, you're too small to fish with that big rod. You stay here and take care of Trixie. Don't let her bark. She scares the fish. We'll be back soon."

"Okay," said Joey.

"And stay in the sun so you'll get dry. If you catch a cold your mother will say it's my fault."

The big boys went upstream, and Joey sat down in the sun. Trixie sat beside him. She put her chin on his knee and went to sleep. Her silky coat was hot from the sun. Joey lay back and looked at the trees and the blue sky. He lay very quietly so as not to disturb Trixie.

After a while the boys came back. Jim had two sunnies and each of the other boys had one. Chuck had caught a frog. When he put it down in the grass Trixie woke up and barked at it. The frog leaped across the grass into the water and Trixie dashed after it. She was going to jump in too, but Joey shouted to her.

"Trixie, come here!" he called.

Trixie trotted back to him and wagged her tail.

"She minds you better than she does me," said Chuck.

Joey felt pleased at that. He thought so too, and he was glad Chuck had noticed it.

"Come on, let's eat," said Jim. "I'm starved."

All the boys except Joey had brought sandwiches. They unwrapped them and began to eat.

Joey watched them for a while. He was pretty hungry too. At last Jim noticed that he was not eating.

"What's the matter?" said Jim. "Didn't you bring any lunch?"

"No," said Joey. "You didn't tell me to."

"Oh, for goodness sake," said Jim, impatiently. "Here, have some of mine."

Joey took the sandwich Jim offered him.

"Here, you can have some of mine too," said Chuck, handing him a cooky.

Bill and Johnny gave him part of their lunch too. Joey began to feel better. The boys really seemed to like him. Now if only he could learn to do the things they did, everything would be all right.

But when they started to play mumblety-peg after lunch, they wouldn't let him play. They said he was too small and might hurt himself with the jackknife.

So Joey threw a stick for Trixie to fetch. She ran after it and grabbed it fiercely in her teeth. She shook it as if it were a dangerous enemy, and brought it back to Joey. He played with her until the boys were ready to start home.

As they walked home through the woods, Joey's rod got caught in the trees a few times, until Jim took it and carried it for him.

25

Joey sighed as he climbed his porch steps.

"Did you catch anything?" his mother asked.

"No, I didn't," said Joey. "The rod fell in the water."

"Well, you *are* a little small for it," said his mother. "But don't be discouraged. You'll get there."

"Sure," said Joey, "I know."

"Here, I made some raisin cookies," said his mother. "Have some."

Joey took three cookies and sat down on the porch to eat them. He tried not to feel discouraged. Maybe next week would be better.

Next week seemed a long way off, but he was so busy at his new school that the time went pretty fast. Before he knew it, it was Saturday again.

Joey looked out of the living-room window. There was Jim coming out with a baseball bat. Joey ran out.

"Hi, Jim," he called. "What are you going to do?"

"Play baseball," said Jim.

Joey remembered that there was a baseball glove in the crate upstairs.

"I have a glove," he said. "Can I go with you?"

"No, you can't," said Jim. "Not today. We're playing in Chuck's yard."

"But, Jim—" Joey began.

"Now, listen," said Jim. "You can't play ball with us. You're too small. We're playing hardball and you might get hurt."

"I could find the ball for you if it gets lost."

"Trixie does that," said Jim. "Look, when I have time I'll go out with you and we'll practice pitching and catching and batting. Then, when you know how, you can play. All right?"

"Okay," said Joey. It was better than nothing.

He watched Jim walk away. Then he went up and looked in the crate. He got out the old baseball glove. He took it downstairs and put it on. It was so big that it wouldn't stay on his hand. He got a piece of string and tied it on. Then he found the rubber ball that Trixie had played with.

He threw the ball against the wall and tried to catch

27

it in his glove. But the big glove just flapped against the
ball and batted it away. He ran after it and threw it again.
This time he managed to catch it. He practiced hard all
morning. By lunch time he could catch most of his throws
if he didn't use the glove too much. The glove was just in
the way. He could really do better without it.

That week Joey practiced every afternoon after school.
He was getting pretty good at throwing and catching.

The next Saturday morning he waited for Jim again.
He had his big glove on his hand. Pretty soon Jim came

out with a glove and a bat, and a baseball in his hand.

"Hi, Jim," said Joey.

"Hi, Joey," said Jim.

"You going to play ball?" Joey asked.

"Yep," said Jim.

"Can I go?"

"Now, listen, Joey," Jim began.

"But I can catch and throw," said Joey. "I practiced all week. Try me."

Jim threw his ball. It was a hard ball, and it stung Joey's hand, even through the glove.

"Ow!" he exclaimed.

"See?" said Jim.

"Well, couldn't I go and play with Trixie?"

"Trixie is missing," said Jim gloomily.

"Missing!" said Joey. "Where?"

"How do I know?" said Jim. "If we knew, she wouldn't be missing. She went off somewhere. She'll be back, I guess."

"Well, maybe I could find lost balls for you," said Joey.

29

Jim apparently couldn't think of any more excuses. "Oh, all right, come along," he said. "But don't get in the way."

"I won't," said Joey. He trotted happily along swinging his glove. Even if he didn't play, he'd learn something by watching. And maybe he'd even get a chance to play. At least he'd be there, and that was better than staying home.

Chuck's yard was wonderful. It stretched from the back porch to some woods that sloped down to the creek. It was really more than a yard. It was a field. In one corner, Chuck's father had built a backstop of chicken wire. In front of this was home plate. First base was over near the back porch. Second base was out toward the woods, and third base was in the far corner.

Chuck, Bill, Johnny and Hank were there when Jim and Joey arrived. There were several other boys too.

"Hi, Jim," they said. Then they looked at Joey. "He can't play. He's too small."

"He's just going to watch," said Jim.

31

"And I'll look for lost balls," Joey promised. "If Trixie isn't back yet."

"No, she isn't," said Chuck. "And I'm worried. I hope nothing's happened to her. She's going to have puppies soon."

"Puppies!" Joey shouted. "Oh, boy! When?"

"I don't know," said Chuck. "In a couple of weeks, I guess."

"Gosh!" Joey sighed. "I wish I could have one."

"Okay," said Chuck. "You find her and I'll give you one. But I doubt if you can find her. We've looked all over. We even called the police this morning. All the neighbors are looking. She must have walked away somewhere and got lost. Or else somebody took her."

Joey was worried. He sat down and tried to figure out where Trixie might be. She couldn't be walking around in the streets because the neighbors would have seen her by this time.

She couldn't be lost, because a smart dog like Trixie just wouldn't go away and get lost.

Maybe she was hurt, and was lying somewhere, unable to come home! Maybe she was caught in a trap somewhere. Joey had read a story about a dog that had stepped into a trap in the woods. But people didn't set traps around here.

Maybe somebody had taken her away, and he would never see her again! This was an awful thought. It just couldn't be. It made Joey feel so sad that he had to think of something else in a hurry, or he might almost cry.

Maybe Trixie was hiding! That was it. But why would she hide? Well, perhaps Chuck's little sister had teased her too much. And if she was going to have puppies, she wouldn't like to be teased. Now the thing to do was to figure out where she would hide.

Joey was thinking so hard that he almost forgot to watch the ball game. Suddenly he realized that Jim was up at the plate. Chuck was pitching for his side. Jim stood with his bat ready, waiting for the pitch. The first one was too high. The next was outside. Then came a couple of strikes.

33

Finally—crack! Jim slammed the ball. He threw down
the bat and ran. The ball flew straight past the second
baseman and rolled toward the woods. The second baseman ran after the ball and Jim galloped around the bases.

34

Joey jumped up and down and yelled, "Home run!
Home run! Go on, Jim! Yay!"

Jim pounded past third base and came into home plate.
Joey threw himself at Jim, yelling, "Hooray! You made it!"

35

"All right, take it easy," said Jim.

"Hey, Chuck," said Johnny. "Trixie always barks when there's a home run, but Joey makes more noise than she does."

"Let's see him find the ball, though," said Chuck.

Joey looked around. He'd been so excited that he had forgotten about hunting the ball. Over among the trees, the second baseman was still looking for it.

Joey tossed his glove on the porch and trotted across the field into the woods. He got a stick and poked about among the bushes. He looked under a rotten log, among some rocks, under the leaves.

"It's no use," said the second baseman, going back to the game. "I've looked everywhere. Take another ball. That one's lost."

Joey stayed in the woods, looking for the ball. He was still wondering where Trixie could be. Maybe she was hiding out here somewhere.

He began to call her softly. "Here, Trixie! Here, girl!"

But there was no answering bark, no scrambling of little paws among the leaves.

But suddenly, as he scuffed along, his foot kicked something. It looked like a rock, but it rolled like a ball. It *was* a ball!

"Here it is!" he shouted, running out on the field with it.

"Good kid!" Jim called back. "Hey, fellows! Joey found the ball. Throw it here, Joey!"

Joey hurled the ball straight across the field to Jim.

"Say, that was a pretty good throw," said Johnny.

"Okay," said Chuck. "You can be the ball boy till Trixie gets back."

37

Joey felt good. He'd found the ball and he'd shown that he could throw. He went and sat down to watch the game.

Jim's team finally struck out and Chuck's side was up at bat. Johnny was first. He was left-handed. After letting a few balls go by, he swung at one and hit it over toward first base. The ball rolled along the ground and took a

little jump on a pebble. The first baseman ran for it, but before he could get to it, it had rolled toward the house and right under the porch.

The porch was so low that it was almost on the ground.

"Now what are we going to do?" said Jim. "Chuck, you ought to have that place screened. The ball's always going under there. We should have Trixie now."

"I'm the ball boy, I'll get it," said Joey.

"You can't get under there," said Chuck.

"Yes, I can," said Joey. He lay down on his stomach and squirmed under the low floor. It smelled of damp,

warm earth. It was warm because the hot sun was shining on the floor over his head. And it was dark. It took a little while for his eyes to get used to the darkness. When he could see, he looked around for the ball. There it was, right in front of him. He wriggled along and got it.

And then he saw something else. Two green spots glowed in the dark. What could they be? Joey remembered a story he had read about a hunter in the jungle who saw two green spots glowing at him, and it had been a tiger. But of course he wasn't in the jungle, and there couldn't be a tiger under the porch floor.

Then he thought, "Maybe a skunk!" Skunks sometimes lived under porches. A skunk would spray him and make him smell. He'd better get out quick.

But of course Trixie wouldn't let a skunk stay there. So it couldn't be a skunk.

"But Trixie is missing!" he said to himself, aloud.

Suddenly there was a little whine from the corner where the spots glowed, and then a little "Woof!"

Why, it was Trixie herself!

"Hey, Trixie!" said Joey. "What are you doing here? Don't you know everybody is looking for you?"

"Woof!" said Trixie again.

She was lying on something that looked like an old sack. Her tail was beating on the ground, thump, thump,

thump! And right beside her on the old sack were three
tiny little things that wiggled and squeaked. Puppies! Trixie
had puppies! She had hidden under the porch and there the
puppies had been born!

Joey patted her. She licked his hand. But when he tried

to touch the puppies, she said, "Woof!" in a warning voice. Joey pulled his hand back.

A ray of sunlight slanted in under the porch so that he could see the puppies. Two were black and the third was brown like its mother.

Joey turned around and wriggled out as fast as he could go. The boys were all standing around the porch waiting for him.

"Here's the ball," said Joey.

"Look at him," said Bill. "Boy, is he dirty!"

"What took you so long?" Jim demanded. "I thought something had happened to you."

"Something did happen," said Joey, "but not to me. Trixie is in there and she has three puppies."

"Trixie is under there!" exclaimed Chuck, grabbing Joey's shoulder. "Are you sure?"

"Of course," said Joey. "She's got an old sack to lie on."

"Let's get her out," said Johnny.

But Chuck shook his head. "No, leave her alone," he said. "She'll come out when she's ready."

"She growled at me," said Joey. "She didn't want me to touch the puppies. I guess she's hiding."

"But why should she hide?" Bill asked.

"Maybe she's afraid my sister will play with the puppies," said Chuck. "But I'm afraid she'll get cold in there."

"No, it's warm," said Joey. "I know what let's do—let's put some food in there so she can eat. She has to eat if she's going to feed the puppies."

"That's a good idea," said Chuck. He went into the house and brought out a dish of meat scraps and a bowl of milk.

45

"Here, Joey," he said, "you're the only one who's small enough to get in there. You crawl in and feed her."

Joey got down on his stomach and pushed the dishes in under the porch. Trixie got up. She came over and drank the milk. She was thirsty. She lapped it all up, and then she put her nose to Joey's ear and licked it. She was saying, "Thank you."

Joey patted her and crawled out. He was very dirty. He wiped his face with his hand and smeared the dirt around.

"Thanks a lot, Joey," said Chuck. "I meant what I said before. You can have one of the puppies."

"Oh, boy!" Joey sighed happily. "And can I be the ball boy till Trixie comes out?"

"You sure can," said Chuck. "And even after that. She'll be too busy with those puppies to chase balls for us."

Joey felt good. "I guess there are some things I'm not too small for," he said.

Jim put his arm around his young cousin. "Know what I think?" he said. "I think he's not too small to play

47

ball right now. Let's put him in the game. Shall we?"

The other boys nodded. "Okay. We'll try him in the outfield."

"Yippee!" Joey yelled. He grabbed his big glove and ran in the direction of the trees. Now if only this glove didn't get in his way and foul things up!

"Wait a minute," Chuck called. "You can't catch anything with that big thing. I'll be right back."

He ran into the house and came back with a little glove. "Try this," he told Joey. "I used to wear it when I was your size."

Joey put the little glove on his left hand. He punched his right fist into it. It was perfect.

"All right, kid," said Jim. "Go on out there."

Joey trotted to the outfield. Jim got ready to pitch. Chuck was up at bat.

"Let's put him out now," Joey shouted.

Jim pitched. Chuck swung and smashed the ball high and far. It soared through the air between first and second base, right toward Joey. Joey put up his hand in the little

glove. He kept his eye on the ball. He ran to meet it.
Smack! The ball met his glove and his other hand

closed over it. Bump! Joey sat down. He held up his left
hand. There was the ball!

51

A yell went up from the boys, "Yay! Joey!" They crowded around and patted him on the back. "Good for Joey," they shouted. "He's in." "You're all right, kid."

Joey grinned. "Thanks," he said.

After the game Joey walked home with Jim. They
didn't say much. They were both tired and hot, but happy.

At the gate, Jim said, "So long, kid. Tomorrow we'll
have some batting practice."

53

"Okay, Jim," said Joey.

He went up to the attic to put away the big glove. He opened the crate and stuffed the glove into a corner. And then he noticed something. It was a small box that he hadn't seen before.

He carried the box to the window and opened it. Inside was a round thing made of leather. It looked like—it was—a dog collar! And there was a leash, and a rubber bone that rattled when he shook it.

"Why, Pop must have had a dog once!" he exclaimed. "I can use these for my dog! He's much too small now for them. But he'll get there."

About the author

Eleanor Clymer has lived in New York all of her life except for her college years at the University of Wisconsin. Well known for her delightful stories for children, she has written during most of her life. But she has also found time to study nursery education and psychology in New York universities and to work with children of various ages at camps and playgrounds. Now that her son, once her severest critic, is of college age, she finds the children of friends an eager jury, always ready with candid opinions on plots and stories.

4546